Hunt
Wi

MW01532912

Characters

Hunter 1

Hunter 2

Hunter 3

Rabbit

Fox

Setting

The woods

Picture Words

box

fishing

Sight Words

go	I	let's	look
now	run	the	will

2

hunting

woods

Enrichment Words

happy	**hear**
ready	**sad**

Hunter 1: We are at the woods. Are you ready to go hunting?

Hunter 2: Yes!

Hunter 3: Let's go.

Hunter 1: Great! A-hunting we will go, a-hunting we will go, hi-ho, the derry-o—

Hunter 3: —a-hunting we will go.

Hunter 2: Go!

Rabbit: Oh no. I hear people. Run!

Fox: I can run. I like to run.

Hunter 2: Look! A fox.

Hunter 3: Get the fox.

Rabbit: Run, Fox, run!

Fox: I am happy to run.

Hunter 3: Get the box.

Rabbit: Go, Fox, go!

Hunter 2: I have the fox!

Fox: Help!

Hunter 1: Put the fox in the box.

Rabbit: Oh no. The fox is in the box.

Fox: Now I can not run. Now I am sad.

Hunter 2: Look.

Hunter 3: The fox is sad.

Hunter 1: The fox is very sad.
Getting the fox was fun.
But I think that letting him go
will be *more* fun.

Hunter 2: Yes!

Hunter 3: Yes! Let the fox go.

Rabbit: Run, Fox, run!

Fox: Now I am happy!

Hunter 1: Hunting *was* fun. Now let's go fishing!

The End

Hunter 1: The fox is very sad. Getting the fox was fun.
But I think that letting him go will be *more* fun.

Hunter 2: Yes!

Hunter 3: Yes! Let the fox go.

Rabbit: Run, Fox, run!

Fox: Now I am happy!

Hunter 1: Hunting *was* fun. Now let's go fishing!

The End